S0-CAJ-628

STEALING FIRE

Writings by Claudia Mauro

STEALING FIRE

Writings by Claudia Mauro

Published in the United States of America
by Whiteaker Press
204 First Avenue South, Suite 3
Seattle, Washington 98104

ISBN 0-9653800-0-9

Stealing Fire by Claudia Mauro © 1996 by Claudia Mauro.
All rights reserved, including the right of reproduction in whole or in part in any form.

CONTENTS

This Book is For

Shelley who pointed towards my voice,
for Tracy who listened,
for BJ's 10 years of harmony,
and for Deborah,
especially for Deborah.

PART

I

THE DAY I STOPPED TAKING MY HEART FOR GRANTED

When I was a little girl, my grandmother taught me that the human heart was a clockworks for angels. She said a person is only given a certain number of heartbeats. The angels keep track and when your heartbeats are all gone, they will come for you. Like all my grandmother's stories, I knew this was true. The proof was everywhere, in the cemetery I passed when I walked to her house, in my grandfather's death, and finally in her own. For a long while I stopped believing in angels, but I never stopped believing that every life is finite, every heart a stopwatch.

Once, I worked out the math: 70 beats a minute = 4200 beats an hour = 100,800 beats a day = 36,792,000 beats a year. 36,792,000 beats a year is an incredible number. It is easy to see how you could take a heart for granted. But despite the equations, the peculiar fact remains that there was a moment when this life ignited like a sun and the heart began beating with the number one, and there will be a moment when the last beat will be counted. The heart will stop, tearing this whole world down with it. I cannot predict that final number, or that final moment, but my heart *will* stop. Forget angels or biology. How can you explain the power and fallibility of a human heart?

One day, when I believed my heart was broken, I decided to take this matter into my own hands. I had a stainless steel .357 magnum revolver called a speed six. I had bought it as a bear gun years before when I lived in Alaska. It had a hatch mark pattern

carved into the grip and across the top of the hammer that made it rough to the touch. The gun was heavy and cold. It glowed with a dull silver sheen. Pulling the trigger with a .357 shell in the chamber created an electric explosion. The force would rock through the body and then a wisp of blue smoke would pour from the barrel. I've heard it said that smoke carries human prayers and thoughts straight to God, so I suppose that revolver was a prayer wheel of sorts.

On that particular day I pulled the gun from its hiding place in my closet and loaded it carefully, slowly. I rolled the bullets between my fingers before I slid them into place. I loaded all six chambers so I could feel the full weight of the thing. My hand felt hollow and empty by comparison.

I brought the barrel up and pressed my temple into the cool steel. My right thumb pulled the hammer back until I heard it click into place. As I ran my finger along the trigger, time began to slow. Traffic and sound on the street below began to freeze. The whole world wound down like movie screen images when a projector slowly stops turning and leaves a single frame suspended, burning away into the glare of a white void.

I turned my head across my shoulder, dragging the gun along my skull. I drew the barrel to a few inches in front of my right eye and stared hard down that black hole. It was the edge of a dark and windy cliff, the whole of eternity packed tight into that four inch by half inch chasm. I decided to pull the trigger.

In the crushing emptiness of that moment there was nothing but one small sound. A faint but

undeniable rhythm, a small pounding, barely heard across a vast distance. It was my heart, and if I was to go any further it would have to be silenced.

I took the gun from my eye and dragged it down across my throat. The hammer was still cocked, my finger still curled around the trigger. I pressed into the barrel just above the center of my left breast but the insistent pounding continued. It was like someone or something knocking hard at a locked door. The knocking grew louder, then something extraordinary happened. My heart, with a bullet packed and ready to explode it apart, gave itself to a perfect, solitary act of bravery— and opened.

The fever broke like shattering glass, an alarm bell roaring. I slowly clicked the hammer back down as time began to move again. The sounds of traffic and human voices poured back into the room. My lungs pulled at the sharp, sweet air as if bursting out from too long under water.

I opened the chamber and let bullets drop onto the wooden floor. They rolled and skittered like scorpions into the darkness behind the radiator and under the bed. (I never did find them all.) I lifted the empty gun up and let sunlight pour through the barrel. Then I put it down and stepped outside into a radiant, magnificent afternoon.

MORNING

Blessed be
this morning
come

The light
inside
the body

THE STAR HUNTER

Deep in the season of Orion
Winter won't wait for Spring.
She draws darkness in around her
and dreams a perfect vision
of crystalline stills.

This is a time to admire
the patience of trees
and the deliberate movements
of the star hunter floating
across her dark and quiet country.

To hurry a change
is to do a kind of violence to a season,
where these snows have
a brief enough moment to glisten,
each one, however bitter or cold,
unique and dazzling as all
that could be delivered
by an early thaw.

Early Autumn, Yukon Territory

Swallows describe God
With aerodynamics
Herons through stillness
Owls in silence.

The Moon has her
Fire opal risings.
Aurora curls firepot red
Across the cool lip of September
While this Earth keeps
Twirling toward morning.

And we, the aboriginal citizens
Of this great blue nation,
Describe God best
When bearing awareness
To the wonder of this
Shimmering world we're born to,
The eyes, mouth and heart
Falling open
Together.

OCTOBER

October is a beautiful word,
like the crack of oak
and frozen gold.

With words like *spring* and *maybe*
only the lips and tongue are wanted,
wanted but not needed.

October requires a commitment
that rolls from the back of the throat,
echoes in the chest and
makes the muscle of a
strong heart ache sweetly.

October holds the smokey distances
of long nights,
the honest work of
a hard love

that stays soft and fluid
when the snows come and
the rivers draw low.

THE ASCENSION

On occasion
a mushroom will shoulder
through asphalt.
Likewise an occasional
blade of grass casts aside
a slab of stone and rises—
not unlike the stories
one hears about Jesus.

And it is every bit
as good a story
and worth celebrating,
even though they
never heard of Jesus
and are only doing
what the living do
when rising
towards light,
against desperate
and impossible odds.

NEWS FROM COLD SPRING

I
In the creek today
the language of water
is heavy with vowels.
Three bubbles spin earthwise,
a translucent prayer wheel
pushing the world forward.

II
There somewhere
off past the edge of you,
those cliffs fall through the edge
of this universe.
Stand and feel
the wind from there!
Ravens dive in
like it was nothing
at all.

III
Those clouds
are the rolling boulders
of northwest November.
The wind keeps busy
quarrying for turquoise.
When she's done,
there will be mist to spin.

IV
Snow,
like its name,
falls silent at the end
of the afternoon.
At twilight,
The Breath
becomes visible.

THE SUN

The sun turns
a field of wheat
gone wild

to cast poems
of moving shadow
written on a road

Wind is the singer
with a raucous
chorus of crows

THE MOON

The moon is tugging on my
heaven strings tonight.
Why are you twinkling at me?

As if you haven't known all along
that we're both made of stars
since before we had skin,
before there was a sky
you knew.

You can afford to twinkle
with nothing to do all night
but reflect that radiance.

Your voice then calls across the water
spilling flocks of silver birds
that light along my body to sing,
"If the blackness is disruptive to you,
I can always pull the shades."

WHAT YOU SEE(K)

Rustle of dry grass
A curved stick
Trickle of flashing water
Tree branches waving
Look for Rattlesnake and
Everything becomes
Rattlesnake.

PRAYER

Hey you,
The One who's dreaming me
I would ask you
to take away what hurts,
but
since it does seem to be
your way of doling
out the unsuspected treasures
you weave of mud and crackling bone,
how about this—

When my heart breaks—
let it break open
and pour it's pinkish light
out onto the way ahead,
to clearly show the carnival
side seductions
I could fall in with,
if there weren't
a glow towards freedom
instead.

PART

II

A Curriculum for Poetry

1. Walk in the October moon.

2. Dream.

3. WAKE UP!

4. Look for the ground luminosity in every living thing, and under the moving marks on paper.

5. Make a rosary out of your scars. Pray it.

6. Make peace with the fact that the sun will explode in 1.1 billion years, melting everything, then shrinking into some kind of dwarf or other, leaving nothing but a bunch of frozen dust floating around in the cold dark.

7. Eat more spinach.

8. Accept the fact that we are all made of stardust and our little lives are held in place by the specific gravity of the stories we spin.

9. Spin a new story.

10. Remember—Truth is heavier than fiction.

11. Tear the hands open and let the heart speak for itself.

12. Love. Love it all. Let its mortality tear the heart to bits. Let go. Then love it all, all over again.

13. When feeling like a fool, strive to be the perfect fool.

14. Descend into hell, but always be home in time for supper.

15. Write it all down.

STEALING FIRE

On nights so dark and lonely
there is no way to know
which is the star
and which the star's reflection
in cold black water,

when terror runs skittering
along the memory
to gnaw through dreams
with the tiny teeth of mice,

and sweat soaked 3 a.m.'s
demand an accounting
for every hot scar
carved inside the skin,

Remember—
this is the cost of stealing fire,
stealing fire back.
Women like us know all about Prometheus
being devoured daily by degrees.

And though you could spend
the life of the body to deny it,
the heart will finally have its say.

Let it rise as radiant heat,
from the flame of a life you can recognize
as undeniably and absolutely
your own.

DAUGHTERS OF TWILIGHT AND DAWN

We walk an edge between the worlds
Between water and mist
Fire and light
This is our song

In your world
There is only
Fire or ice
Earth or air
Woman or man

While we, the daughters of twilight and dawn
Slip silent between the worlds
Between the wing and the weather
The wind and the wave

The alchemical animals of our eyes
Burn with starlight and spirit
Dreams and desire
You look straight at us but don't see

Past the manicured garden
In the wildwood
We wear a robe of two spirits
Warp of dark
Weft of light side of moon

If you heard us
Dancing on the edge
Of spark to flame
Our hearts thrown open
In a moonlight howl —
Would your body betray you?

You frighten so easily
Defined by shadow
In a world all dark or light
Black or white
You pray we aren't kindred
But you need us
More than you think

We remember our real names
We know the way home
We are your guides
This is our song

EVOLUTION OF TOOLS (for Tracy)

Whenever I see rust
I think of you.
This is not some poem
about being old and worn.
This is a poem
about the evolution of tools
and the magnetics of an eye
that gathers them
from freeway ditches and
back alley exile.
Those that were forsaken
come to be of use again.

Old wrenches,
a rail car spring,
anchor chains,
and various nails
have relaxed their grip
and become blind prophets
huddled around your door.
Prodigal voices
run together in the rain,
call up an ultimate
elemental value

When every evening
along stone steps
the rust remembers
and in chorus roars,
A woman's blood
is made of iron and
her heart a foundry hammer.
Sniff the rain but
keep on climbing,
and that heavy, working patience
will carry you
finally home.

THE DIFFERENCE BETWEEN ME AND HER

The roofers next door
Started at seven.
She got up,
Made strong coffee.

I stayed in bed
And dreamt
Of immense
Woodpeckers.

TIDE TABLE

A moon
is more persistent
than the best of intentions.
A promise to hold the tide—
always a lie.

The truth is
when you speak
the wind stills.
I watch your mouth move—
words float by, half heard
buzz against my skin.
When you laugh
the ceiling cracks and
the sky arcs open impossibly blue.
When I dream,
you curl around the edge
of my wishes and vanish
soft as a whispered prayer,
an opening eye.

Now I live by the ocean,
which is a good place to cry.
A woman wants to feel
like she's filling something
while she watches
a lover fade in daylight
like a star.

LIVING TWICE

Living twice today
I got out of bed
on two separate occasions.

Once, I stroked her hair
kissed her cheek
and said,
Good morning.

Once, I stroked her hair
kissed her cheek
and said,
Good bye.

BULIMIA BLUES

Come on baby.
Why don't you just crawl
over here and lick me.

I'm all the sugar
soft darkness
you crave.

Later I'll push
my bitter finger down
over your voice
and pull all your
inside out.

I'll drive you so hard
beat you so complete
beat you so deep,

Till you can say
the bleeding *yes*
to anybody's hands on you.

Compared to me,
they'll be so gentle
and so sweet.

AFTER YOU'RE GONE

I can't reach the moon
but I can feel it pull.

I can't see the wind
But I am still breathing.

I can't see my heart
but I know the curve of your breast
under my fingertip,
as real as this earth spinning round,

Even though your body isn't really you
and my body isn't really me,
but more like a signpost
marking time and distance
to an invisible world,

Where rain made of light
dissolves everything
we think we know
and everyone we think we are
into a river made of grace.

And nothing is left
but a scissor tailed trace of memory—
the way the presence of swallows
lingers in a late autumn sky.

THE EMPTY ROOM

What finally drove me to my knees
was that late May afternoon.

The impression your body had left
on the down comforter
was so soft, no edges,
no edges at all.

The empty room
was warm and light.
For a moment my body rose
to trace a memory of you
quiet and asleep in my arms.

That's when
I finally fell forward
and down,
to watch particles of dust
suspended in sunlight,
gently settle over the place you had been.

Turn of Weather

She says
she doesn't like
her name and invites you
to prove her wrong.

Meanwhile,
to just say
she is beautiful
would be like saying
the first lowland snow
of a dark and lovely December
is just so much cold air and water,
an ordinary turn of weather.

It is hard to look directly at her,
like snow in sunlight.
She's been lied to so often
she'll believe anything,
and if she catches you
breathless and transfixed—

I mean
if she glimpses
her radiance reflected
in your eyes—
she'll mistake you for the enemy
for daring to love her.

INVOLUNTARY REFLEX

She was worried
about what might happen
and said so

looking at that love
through binoculars
held backwards

so that everyone
in the future
looked smaller

of course we knew
what would happen
the way one unspoken word

leads to the next
It couldn't be helped
like breathing in and out

now I think it's funny,
how you can't keep
from blinking without crying

funny,
how the valves of the heart
open and close

THE WAY SHE MOVES

The way she moves

    Silk

       Fire

          Light across the wall

The way she moves

    The way she moves

        The way she moves

Do You Want Anything?

That winter I had a dream. There was a deep forest lake. The water level had risen and drowned the young trees at the water line. I couldn't say why the water level had risen—maybe a dam or a landslide. Perhaps a memory had fallen across the outflow hoping to slide unnoticed beneath the surface. This was after all a dream.

The trees were stark, bleached skeletons scattered against a gray sky. Branches flung out from their trunks as if death by drowning had frozen them in surprise. Some had fallen into the dark, green water. Snags were everywhere.

I was with her on the muddy bank. We had come to swim. We faced each other and began walking sideways into the water, each mirroring the movements of the other. She swam ahead of me with sure strokes that barely rippled the surface. Her dark hair glistened in the grey light. I followed, the murky bottom falling out from under my feet as the water turned deeper, colder.

She swam toward a half sunken building near the middle of the lake, a cafe. The cafe was deserted but half submerged vending machines still glowed and whirred. She turned her back to me and planted her feet firmly on the cafe's underwater floor. She began popping quarters in a Coke machine that had a red and white glow. I was treading water.

"Do you want anything?" she asked.

My foot caught in a snag. I thought 'I should ask for something, I might drown,' but I was oddly calm.

"Do you want anything?" she asked again. She didn't turn around. The snag became a hand, gripped

my foot tighter and tried to pull me under. I looked down and saw what might have been a face, transient and pale.

"Do you want anything?" Her voice was low and soft.

'I should ask for something,' I thought again, 'I will drown,' but the strange calm continued and I was silent. My nose and throat began to fill with green water. The dark, velvety liquid streamed through my fingers.

"Do you want anything?" I heard her ask once more. The hand clamped down harder and pulled. I sputtered and kicked, my foot broke free. I swam hard for shore, but found the bottom under my hip. I never asked for anything, and she never turned around.

PART

III

Solitary Memory is Not Enough

It's hard to know where to begin. The story starts and ends in so many places. I suppose I could begin by telling you about the cemetery. There was a light rain, everywhere the sound of raindrops falling on blades of grass, pine boughs, granite and bronze. The sound was like muffled applause or the soft murmuring of an unseen crowd. Birds were quietly chattering among themselves. Judging by their subdued voices, I guessed it was about to start raining harder. Birds know when the weather is about to change. If you ask them by offering your quiet attention, they will always tell you.

It was a nice place really, a churchyard at the top of a hill that slopes gently upward through two miles or so of farms and open meadows. The fields were green and brown. It was early August. Enormous bales of freshly cut hay filled the air with a deep summer scent. I nestled under an old Doug fir by the graves of my friends.

David S. Chance	Stephen C. Brunner
Beloved	Beloved Son and Brother
Feb. 5, 1951 - Apr 22, 1987	Sept. 6, 1952 - Nov 20, 1990

The markers were gray granite about two feet high. I didn't know Lopez Island very well, and I was afraid that I wouldn't be able to find my way. Intuition and a Kestrel pointed me right to the cemetery though, no wrong turns. I had been there only once before, a hot August afternoon six years ago. It was the day Stephen took me to see David's grave.

Buried about one third of its height in front of David's stone was a pitcher, an old cream colored ceramic pitcher like the kind you'd see with a porcelain wash

basin. It had a light brown handle that had been carefully glued back in place and a pattern of green ivy leaves painted on the front. It was for holding flowers I supposed. There was more to it than that though. Something about David and antiques, something about that pitcher in particular, something just beyond the reach of my memory. So the story is lost.

When I first got there, the pitcher was filled with dirt, pine needles and cobwebs. It hadn't held flowers for a long time. No one had been there for a long time. None of David's family would have ever been there. "They were Christians" Stephen said. "They abandoned David when he got sick."

As for Stephen's family, I didn't know. The stone they carved him said, 'Beloved son and brother.' They didn't mention the word, 'lover.'

All around the pitcher, David's gravestone, and the grave itself, were small rocks and shells that were clearly brought from somewhere else. Stephen told me he would bring them. They were all half buried under dust and pine needles. There were pinkish orange rocks, green speckled ones, white quartzite, hermit crab shells, all carefully selected and placed. They weren't obvious. If you didn't know someone used to come and bring them, you probably would have missed them. They were brighter in the rain, probably chosen from the tide line while they were wet and shiny. There were no rocks or shells around Stephen's grave.

A drop of rain hit the pitcher just right, and made a perfect pinging sound, like a tiny bell. I looked up from my notebook for that. After all, hundreds of thousands of raindrops had fallen, but just this one made that pitcher sing. I wish I could remember the pitcher story. A story, no matter how small, shouldn't just be lost like

that. But it had been six years since Stephen told me the story and my solitary memory is not enough.

What can I tell you about Stephen? I met him in 1980. We worked as shipping and receiving clerks at a small outdoor equipment mail order house. I was just coming out then, but I remember Stephen was so good looking that he sort of confused me. He was a huge, baby blue eyed former 'Mr. International Leather.' He loved to gossip. During breaks we would sit on the loading dock while he amazed me with tales of his after hours adventures. In a world of 'wanna be's,' he was a *genuine* sexual outlaw and my first openly gay pal.

I remember one summer afternoon in particular. The heat in the warehouse was stifling. We passed the time with jokes and chatter, talked about a few of his most recent tricks. We talked about STDs.

I remember him saying, "Yeah, the ones before me got it and the ones after me got it. I didn't. It's always been that way. I'm just strong and lucky I guess. I never get sick." He laughed. We were talking about hepatitis then.

I had this thing with Stephen. It's hard to explain. In the years that followed I was in and out of Seattle. I wouldn't see him, sometimes for years at a time. Then a silent alarm would start to go off somewhere in between my heart and intuition, and I'd just know it was time to call Stephen or for him to call me. We had the kind of connection where we could go a year or two without talking and then just pick it up again without skipping a beat.

In 1982, he told me he had met a man named David. He had fallen deeply in love and had decided to become a 'housewife.' I was shocked. I said, "Come on Steve, you have *got* to be kidding. . . you? . . . married?"

"It's true," he said. "We just bought land up on Lopez. We're going to build a house."

"Wow," I said. "I gotta meet *this* boy."

In 1985, Stephen told me that David had gotten sick. They had to give up building the house. "It's hard to hold up your end of the sheet rock when you weigh a hundred pounds." Steve said.

When I first met David he was 200 lbs of muscular athlete. The last time I saw him, a fall night in 1986, he was gray and drawn. He weighed 90 lbs. and couldn't sit up by himself. His eyes were sunken, and his skin was stretched papery thin across his face. All the bones of his skull were clearly visible. There was a certain smell in the room, pungent and dark.

As I sat by his grave, I remembered the November evening that I last saw David. It was unusually cold that night. The two of them lived in a small rented cottage above Lake Washington. I was sitting on the edge of David's bed chatting, when it started to snow. David was looking past me, past the photographs of the handsome, strong, sparkling eyed man whose face shone out from the bedroom walls. He was gazing out the window with a distracted and delighted look on his face. The snow swirled around the street lights. "Excuse me," he finally said. "It's snowing. I love snow. I don't know if I'll ever see it snow again." A few months later David was dead.

It is hard to remember snow in early August. It was hard to believe that eight years had passed since that night.

The next day on Lopez Island dawned sunny and clear. The rainstorm broke sometime during the night. The morning was warm and beautiful. A sunny summer day after a rain is such a luxurious thing. All the wildflowers turned toward the sunlight like a million freshly

washed faces. The roadsides were covered with deep pink foxgloves. I was going to pick some to put in the pitcher, but I just couldn't pick a flower on a day like that.

I didn't get back to the cemetery till early afternoon. I thought about the day Stephen showed me David's grave. It was deep summer then too. First, we drove to a park, Shark Reef point, and sat by the water. Stephen was drinking a bottle of champagne. He said he didn't think he would be able to come to that place again after David's death. It was a special place for them. "But," he said, "time and the champagne takes the sting out some."

He was worried about his drinking, especially right after. He went to a recovery group for a while, but gave it up. He said, "Being listened to is such a powerful thing for a lonely person, . . . but you know how they say this recovery stuff will ruin your drinking?"

"Yeah," I said, "I knew."

"Well I don't want my drinking ruined just yet." We laughed.

Then Steve told me about the day he buried his lover. "We were afraid the locals might not want David buried here, but it wasn't a problem." In fact, some local friends who Stephen described as 'very hunky' helped him carry the coffin which was wrapped in leather straps. He told me, "David would have *loved* that. He *loved* to be all tied up."

Stephen said he got in the grave and lowered one end of the casket in. The moment the corner of the casket touched the earth, he said he felt a wave of relief and peace flood through him. "We did it!" he said aloud to David, "We made it!" He looked up to see a rainbow in the fields below on that late April afternoon.

He told me about the night David died. He had been in the hospital for about a week. A roller coaster of

dementia, seizures, and high fevers. He said, "The nurses would meet me at the elevator sometimes. He could get so out of control. That night was bad. After awhile though, he calmed down for a minute and showed up, all David. He looked at me and said, 'I love you,' then fell into a coma. I got in bed and held him till I fell asleep.

"At about 2 am, the nurse woke me up, and gently whispered, 'He's gone . . . take as much time as you need.' Then she left. I looked at David's face and thought, 'He doesn't look dead. He still looks like David.' I held him.

"Then something began to happen. The room began to fill with something like tiny sparks, fireflies, filaments of light, all in motion. Sort of like the sunlight on the tide there, but more brilliant and blindingly beautiful.

"The light became intense and suddenly we were in motion on this river of gold lights. We drifted through the hospital walls. I remember thinking, 'They're going to be surprised to find us gone when they look in the room.' The river kept moving faster and getting bigger. I had to hold on tight to David. The speed was incredible! Suddenly, I sort of got kicked back into an eddy and David flew out of my arms. Then I was back on the AIDS ward again.

"I looked at David's body and thought, '*Now* he's dead.' Bits of that river clung to me. The feeling was indescribable. The peace! In the halls, the nurses stopped talking and stared at me. They could see the filaments too. I knew I would never be afraid of death again."

Sometime in 1991, I got that feeling. Time to call Stephen. A voice I didn't recognize answered the phone. I asked for Stephen. After a long pause, the voice said,

"Stephen Brunner? . . . He died about a year ago . . . Yeah, I think he was buried on Lopez." The voice told me his name, but my ears were ringing and I didn't hear him. He said he just happened to be there cleaning up the place. He told me his best friend Bill was living there when Stephen died. Bill could have told me more about it, he said, but Bill died last Saturday. His voice cracked.

So I don't know the details of how Stephen died. All I know is that he didn't die ashamed or afraid.

Now it's August 1994, and I just came to visit. I found a 'Sacred Heart of Mary' novena candle with a bar code sticker just under the seraphim at the local store. I thought, "Well the boys will appreciate that."

I collected some special rocks and a broken shell at Shark Reef point. I put the novena candle between them, and said a rosary. I arranged the rocks and shell around Stephen's grave and said, "These are from David."

I took an eagle feather I found by the graves and a nylon rainbow bracelet a friend brought me from the Lesbian and Gay March on Washington and hung them around Stephen's grave with a long string. I took a heart a friend had woven out of three reeds and hung it around David's grave. I told them, "On Gay Pride Day this year, a rainbow flag a mile long marched down the center of Manhattan Island to the Stonewall. It's been 25 years." I want to believe that matters.

I remember shipping and receiving. Stephen would breeze by me grinning and say, "I'd love to kiss ya, but I just washed my hair." He'd wink over his shoulder and vanish around a corner.

I wiped the dust from the pitcher, cleaned out the cobwebs. I left the dirt and pine needles. I tore a sheet from my notebook and wrote, 'LOVER AND BELOVED,' and pushed it deep inside the pitcher, into the dirt and fresh rainwater.

You Wouldn't Think

You wouldn't think
It would be so easy
To forget
Who we really are

Or that death is always at our shoulder
Or that everything is alive
Or that God is everywhere singing

About the Author

Ms. Mauro is, among other things, a first generation New York Italian Amazon leather Buddhist butch in recovery. She holds Federal Aviation Administration Commercial Pilot Certificate number 131407693, and certainly knows how to stall *and* how to recover.

Since her first writing class she has simplified her life to include just two activities—writing and not writing. Her goal is to embody the sacred, the profane and the moment they ride in on.*

*This final preposition is dedicated to Shelley.

NOTES ON THE BOOK DESIGN

Book cover is 80 lb. Fox River Confetti. Hand mounted title inset is 70 lb Hopper Proterra. Inside stock is Simpson Evergreen Recycled. All paper used is 100% recycled with 50% post-consumer-waste.

Cover and inside text was set in Agaramond and Wood Ornaments, both from Adobe Type. Agaramond is a recasting of the old serif type face Garamond, originally designed in the 16th century by Claude Garamond. The new Adobe Agaramond was designed by Robert Slimbach in 1989. The Wood Ornament font was developed in 1990 by the Adobe Type Design Team using research from 19th century industrial styles of wood block prints.

Book design by Tracy Lamb, Seattle, Washington.